The SIXTEEN HAND Horse

written and illustrated by

FRED GWYNNE

Windmill/Wanderer
Books
New York

Copyright © 1980 by Fred Gwynne

Published by Windmill Books Inc. and Wanderer Books
A Simon & Schuster Division of Gulf & Western Corporation
Simon & Schuster Building 1230 Avenue of the Americas New York, New York 10020

Library of Congress Cataloging in Publication Data
Gwynne, Fred.   The sixteen hand horse.
SUMMARY: Depicts a little girl's visual images of her parents' talking
about such things as bells that peel, banking a fire,
and a running nose.
1. English language—Homonyms—Juvenile literature. [1. English language—Idioms,
corrections, errors. 2. English language—Homonyms] I. Title.
PE1595.G8   428'.1   79-13284
ISBN 0-671-96100-4

Designed by The Etheredges
Manufactured in the United States of America
1 2 3 4 5 6 7 8 9 10

for D.F.G.

Mommy says that she wants a horse that is sixteen hands.

Mommy says

puppies should be
paper trained.

Mommy says that
  churches have cannons...

...and bells

that peel.

Daddy _____ knows a man

who fought a suit and lost.

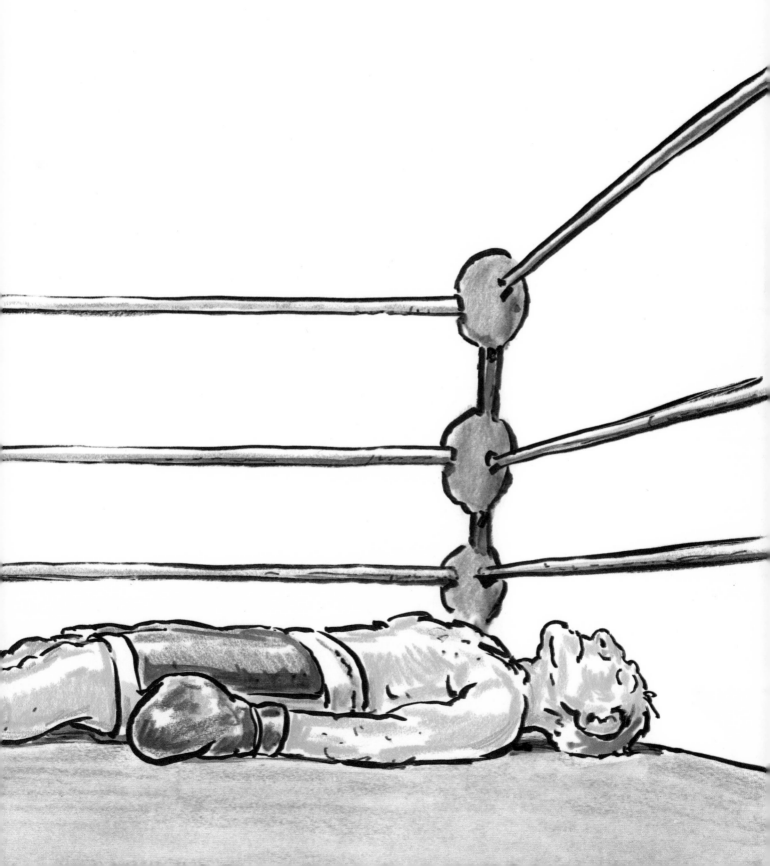

Daddy says Uncle Arthur

runs a plant...

And they live in an eary house.

Mommy says she and Daddy
went to the opera and

were moved by the orchestra.

And sat in a tear.

Daddy says he caught
a fish on a spoon.

Mommy says
   her nose is running.

Daddy says his car
has a crack in its block.

It says on the radio to

watch out for a rabbit dog.

Daddy says  there are locks

big enough to hold a battleship.

Daddy says he won't

join the tennis club, because
all the members are wasps.

Daddy says once he knew
a soldier who was

a wall.

Mommy asked the grocer

to see his fish row.

Daddy says he's going to bank

the fire.

Daddy says he won't play cards

if the steaks are too high.

Daddy says a hunting dog can flush a pheasant.